MICROSCOPIC Milton

**For Oscar
and Amy**

MILTON AND THE DUST COLLECTION

WRITTEN BY TONY GARTH
ILLUSTRATED BY IAN JACKSON & TONY GARTH

© SPLASH! Holdings Limited. 1996. Printed in Hong Kong.
Typography and typesetting - Metcalf & Poole, Leeds, England.

It was a very quiet afternoon and as usual Douglas the dog was asleep in front of the fire.

The only sound that could be heard was the gentle ticking of the old clock on the mantelpiece. This particular old clock was very special indeed, it was the home of Microscopic Milton.

Inside the clock, Milton was spending a very enjoyable time looking through his collection of dust.

Milton had a very impressive collection of rare dust from all over the world, which had taken him years to find. There was blue speckled dust from the jungles of Africa, volcanic dust from tropical islands and a shiny, black piece of coal dust from the very first steam engine.

But Milton's favourite and most precious piece was a speck of gold dust which his great, great grandfather had collected when he was still a young man.

Milton's great, great grandfather, Minuscule Montgomery had been a great explorer and Milton loved to tell Douglas about his adventures. His favourite story was about how his great, great grandfather found the priceless gold dust in an old abandoned mine shaft, and had to battle with snakes and scorpions before he finally recovered it and brought it home.

'It must be very exciting to be a great explorer and adventurer,' thought Milton.

Suddenly the peace was shattered by a terrible noise and the clock began to shake.

'What on Earth is that?' thought Milton as he carried his precious gold dust outside onto the mantelpiece to investigate. He looked down to see Mrs Witherspoon wrestling with a brand new 'Turbo Deluxe' high power vacuum cleaner which was completely out of control! Douglas hid behind a chair as Mrs Witherspoon tried to pull the vacuum nozzle away from the carpet, it was sucking so hard that it would hardly move!

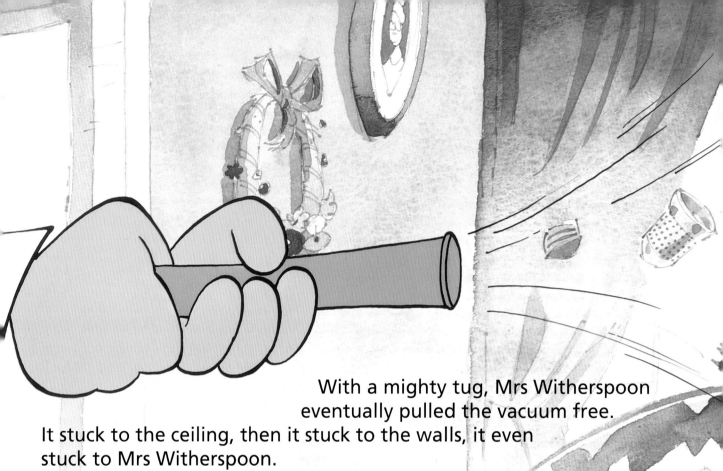

With a mighty tug, Mrs Witherspoon
eventually pulled the vacuum free.
It stuck to the ceiling, then it stuck to the walls, it even
stuck to Mrs Witherspoon.

'It's alive!' she shrieked as the vacuum cleaner sucked up
everything in its path; ornaments, dried flowers, an odd glove and
an entire quarter pound of mint humbugs all disappeared
up the tube.

Milton stared in amazement as the nozzle of the
vacuum cleaner swung round towards him. 'Oh no!' he
shouted as the gold dust was sucked from his hand. He
tried to run away but it was too late and Milton
disappeared down the long tube and followed the dust
into the vacuum cleaner.

Mrs Witherspoon eventually managed to find the switch and turn off the machine. 'Goodness me!' she said 'I'm exhausted. There is definitely something wrong with this contraption and I'm going to telephone the shop right now and tell them so.' As soon as Mrs Witherspoon had left the room, Douglas came out from behind the chair and looked down the tube into the vacuum cleaner but he couldn't see any sign of Milton He was very worried.

'Woof!' he shouted to Milton and waited for a reply.

'I'm all right,' said a tiny voice from inside.

It was very dark inside the vacuum cleaner and Milton could hardly see a thing. 'There must be lots of useful things in here', he thought and began to search through the fluff and debris until he found what he was looking for.

Milton found a light bulb from a Christmas tree, a tiny battery, some bits of wire and a bottle cap from which he made what looked like a miners helmet with a lamp on the front.

'That's better', he said to himself, 'now I can see where I'm going and I can search for my priceless speck of gold dust.'

Milton found an old toothpick and began to fight his way through the fluff. 'This must be what it feels like to be a great explorer and adventurer,' thought Milton, 'but without the scorpions and snakes, thank goodness.'

Suddenly Milton heard a rustling sound behind him and quickly turned around to see a giant, hairy spider staring straight at him, at least it seemed like a giant to someone of Miltons size.

Milton gulped and then he noticed something glint in the light from his helmet. 'It's my gold dust', he shouted, and so it was. Unfortunately the spider was standing right on top of it.

'Now, what would my great, great grandfather have done in a situation like this?' thought Milton as he looked around for something to scare the spider away with.

The spider moved slowly towards Milton but before it knew what was happening, Milton had found an old fountain pen and was squirting bright green ink straight into the spider's face. The spider scuttled away in fright and Milton felt very brave as he picked up his gold dust and put it safely in his pocket.

Meanwhile, Douglas was carefully examining the buttons on top of the vacuum cleaner trying to find a way to rescue his friend inside.

'I wonder what this one is for?', he thought and decided to press it to find out. There was a loud buzzing and rattling. 'Oh no', thought Douglas, 'Now what have I done?,' Douglas had switched the vacuum to blow instead of suck. All the dust and fluff was blown out into the room in great billowing clouds and so was Microscopic Milton who landed safely onto a soft cushion.

'Thanks Douglas', said Milton, 'just wait until I tell you about my adventure.' Before he had a chance, the parlour door opened and in came Mrs Witherspoon with the man from the vacuum cleaner shop. She couldn't believe her eyes, the room was covered from floor to ceiling in dirt. 'Just look at this mess,' she shouted at the man, 'your silly vacuum cleaner has done this, I told you it was faulty'.

Mrs Witherspoon went to fetch her reliable, old vacuum cleaner from under the stairs. She then made the man from the shop clean up every last speck of dirt with it before taking the new one away with him.

Milton and Douglas crept outside and hid in the garden shed for a few hours until Mrs Witherspoon had calmed down.

'Have I told you everything about my adventures with the giant spider?' asked Milton. 'Three times today already,' thought Douglas as he settled down to hear them again.

In the distance he heard a faint scream as Mrs Witherspoon discovered a bright green spider in her kitchen.